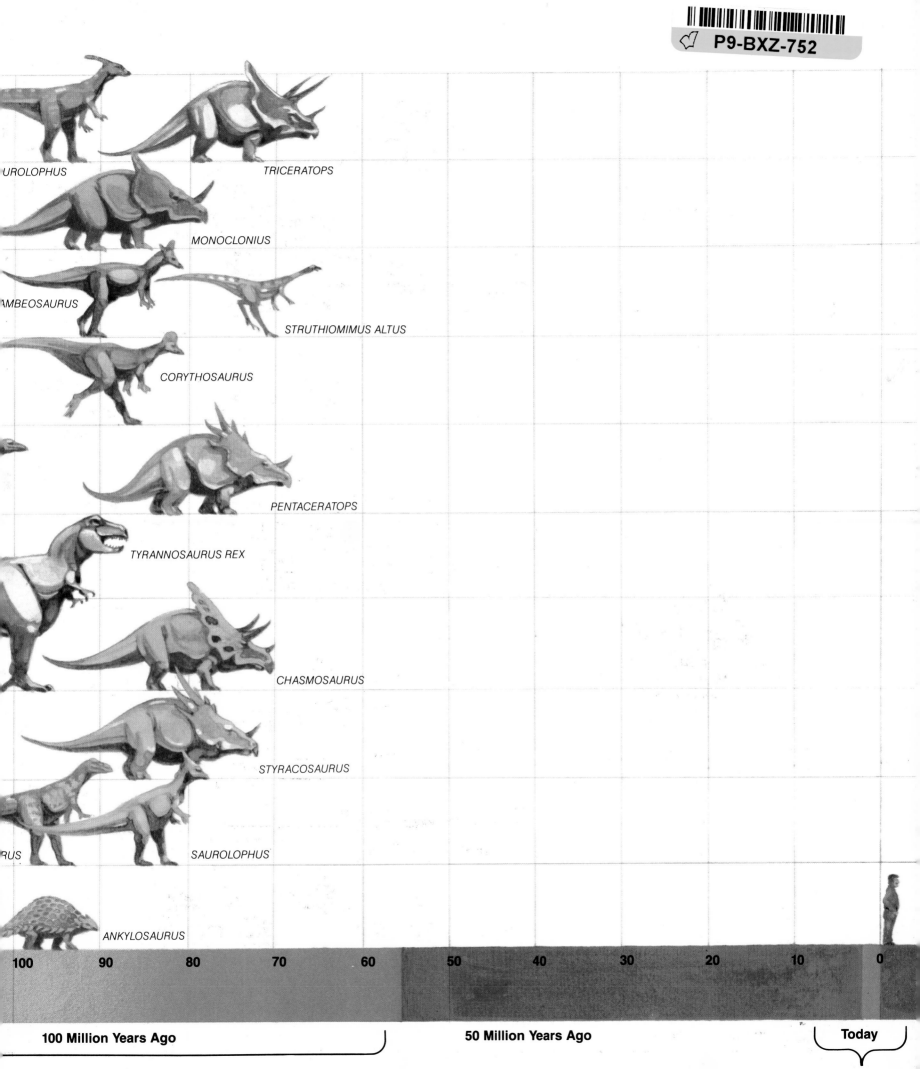

UROLOPHUS

TRICERATOPS

MONOCLONIUS

AMBEOSAURUS

STRUTHIOMIMUS ALTUS

CORYTHOSAURUS

PENTACERATOPS

TYRANNOSAURUS REX

CHASMOSAURUS

STYRACOSAURUS

RUS   SAUROLOPHUS

ANKYLOSAURUS

| 100 | 90 | 80 | 70 | 60 | | 50 | 40 | 30 | 20 | 10 | 0 |

100 Million Years Ago   **50 Million Years Ago**   **Today**

Age of Man

For Cara, Christy, and their Uncle Walter—three very special omnivores.

To Jamie and Miranda

ACKNOWLEDGEMENTS

New and exciting theories about the fundamental nature of dinosaurs have recently been advanced by Adrian J. Desmond and John H. Ostrom, two of the most original and brilliant people in the field of paleontology. I relied heavily on their research to include in *Dinosaurs* the most accurate information to date.

John C. McLoughlin's creative and imaginative writing coupled with his lyrical illustrations brought these amazing creatures to life for me.

I owe a special thanks to geologist Richard Krueger of Dinosaur Park, Hartford, CT, whose careful review of my manuscript proved invaluable.

Library of Congress Cataloging in Publication Data

Packard, Mary.   The dinosaurs.
SUMMARY: An introduction to dinosaurs, in question-and-answer format, with illustration, time line, and atlas.
1. Dinosaurs—Juvenile literature. [1. Dinosaurs—Miscellanea.
2. Questions and answers]
I. Santoro, Christopher, ill, II. Title.
QE862.D5P13   567.9'1   81-16870
20 19 18 17 16 15 14
ISBN 0-671-43040-8

DINOSAURS

Text by Mary Packard   **Illustrations by Christopher Santoro**

SIMON AND SCHUSTER BOOKS FOR YOUNG READERS
Published by Simon & Schuster, Inc., New York

What was the world like when the dinosaurs (DI-no-sores) were still around?

The first dinosaurs lived 200,000,000 years ago, before there was such a thing as a person. It's hard to understand how long ago that time really was. Maybe the time line at the beginning of this book will help you. That tiny little section far to the right shows you how long—actually, how short—a time man has been on earth.

Let's pretend you have a magic time machine. You press a button and it will take you back to that long-ago time when the dinosaurs roamed the earth. As you land, you find yourself on a sandy beach before a warm, shallow ocean. The swampy jungle, to either side of you, is full of trees and plants you've never seen before.

In among all this greenery are some dinosaurs, enjoying a snack of plant leaves.

The only things that don't look new are the spiders, dragonflies, cockroaches, and turtles. Oh, yes, there are also crocodiles. Their know-it-all grins seem to be saying that they intend to be around for a long, long time.

If dinosaurs lived before human beings were around to describe them in books, how do we know about them?

The answer to that question is "bones." Certain scientists called paleontologists (pay-lee-on-TOL-o-jists) spend their lives looking for not only bones, but footprints, and teeth as well. They call them fossils. Fossils are what we need to prove that these strange creatures really stalked the earth.

What do paleontologists do with the fossils they find?

Because they know so much about bones, they are able to figure out how the dinosaur bones fit together to form a skeleton. This skeleton gives them a pretty good idea of what the dinosaur looked like when it was alive.

Does that mean that their work is finished?

Not at all. Now the mystery story really begins. Why are the teeth so long and sharp? The better to grind up their prey, perhaps? Why are the bones hollow? The better to get away in a hurry? (The lighter you are, the faster you run.)

Each body part is another clue to the way the dinosaur lived and died. As you read about each dinosaur, look for clues. See if you can help solve some of the mysteries. Don't be surprised if a clue leads you to more questions than you had to begin with.

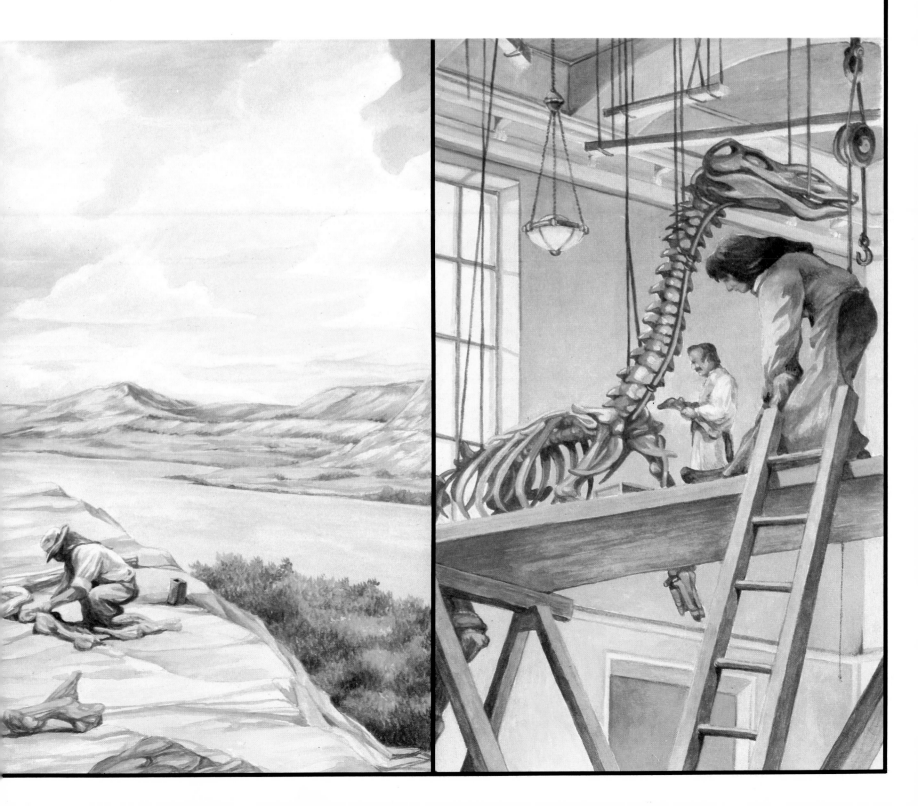

Coelurasaurus

Were dinosaurs reptiles?

Some paleontologists say yes; some say no. A reptile is an animal whose body is covered with layers of hard spots called scales. Snakes, crocodiles, and lizards are a few reptiles you already know about. Since reptiles can't heat their own blood, the sun has to do it for them. So they spend a lot of time sunbathing to get the energy to move. Scales are especially good for soaking up heat. Without heat, reptiles are like toys with dead batteries. That's why they're called cold-blooded animals.

Were all the dinosaurs big?

Huge, scary, slow ... These are words that some people might use to talk about dinosaurs. Before they knew about Coelurosaur (se-LUR-a-sore) dinosaurs, that is. Once they saw a picture of a Coelurosaur, they would want to choose other words like small, thin, and graceful.

Coelurosaurs were carnivores (CAR-ni-vors). That means that they ate meat. They walked on two legs with their tails held stiffly in the air. On their very strong legs, they could run fast enough to catch smaller animals and get away from larger ones. This leads us to another very important question.

How many hours in the sun would it take to make a Coelurosaur run?

None. Most scientists think that the speedy Coelurosaurs were warm-blooded, so they wouldn't need to sunbathe for energy like cold-blooded crocodiles would. They ask, "Why would a body built to run long distances need to lie in the sun all day so that it could move?"

Saltopusuchus

Beep! Beep! Who was that?

That must have been Saltopusuchus (salt-o-po-SOOK-us), a Coelurosaur whose name means "leaping foot." His footprints tell us that he moved more like a roadrunner than a kangaroo. A little guy, he was about the size of your pet cat with a long, thin neck like a swan.

Coelophysis

Where did the speedy Coelurosaurs get their energy?

They never stopped eating. Coelophysis (see-lo-FEE-sis), for example, was always looking for a meal. She was about the size of a greyhound and almost as fast. Her jaws lined with teeth like steak knives made an excellent trap for catching smaller animals. Watch out, Saltopusuchus!

Compsognathus

Where is a good place to find a Compsognathus (comp-so-NA-thus)?

Inside the body of another Compsognathus! And that is precisely the place where paleontologists discovered the bones of this little creature. They were resting inside the skeleton of a Coelurosaur that looked exactly like him.

Compsognathus is one of the smallest dinosaurs that we know about. No bigger than a crow, this little glutton would chomp on any animal he could get his hands on, including it seems, some of his best friends!

Struthiomimus Altus

Which was the fastest Coelurosaur?

If there were a dinosaur Olympics, Struthiomimus Altus (stroo-thee-o-MY-mus AL-tus) surely would have won the gold medal in every running event. His very long, powerful legs must have made him one of the fastest creatures that ever lived. His name means "ostrichlike."

Instead of a strong jaw with sharp teeth, this dinosaur had a beak like the birds you see today. (Scientists think he ate the eggs of other dinosaurs.) About as tall as a man with a long neck and big eyes, he really did look a lot like an ostrich.

Archaeopteryx

Did any dinosaurs have feathers?

When tiny Archaeopteryx (ar-kay-OP-tur-iks) died, he had no idea that he would be giving away some very important secrets about himself to us, creatures living so many millions of years after him. Just after he died, mud dried around his body. The mud turned to stone so that we now have a perfect picture of him. When scientists study the picture, they see a skeleton made just like other Coelurosaurs except for two amazing things. Archaeopteryx had feathers and a wishbone!

Was Archaeopteryx the first bird that every lived?

Could be. Scientists had already noticed that Coelurosaur skeletons and bird skeletons were very much alike.

We can tell from footprints that Coelurosaurs and birds had the same kind of feet and that they both walked standing up. One thing Archaeopteryx couldn't do was flap his wings. We know this because his skeleton is missing the special bones that birds need for flying.

What did Archaeopteryx need feathers for?

Perhaps they were there to help keep his small body warm. Maybe he stretched out his arms to catch a breeze so his feathers could help him glide from one rock to another. Or his feathers might have helped him steer so he could make sharp turns while he was running.

These are things we can only guess about. Don't you think it's fun to imagine that the little bird outside your window might be the only living relative of what was once the mighty dinosaur?

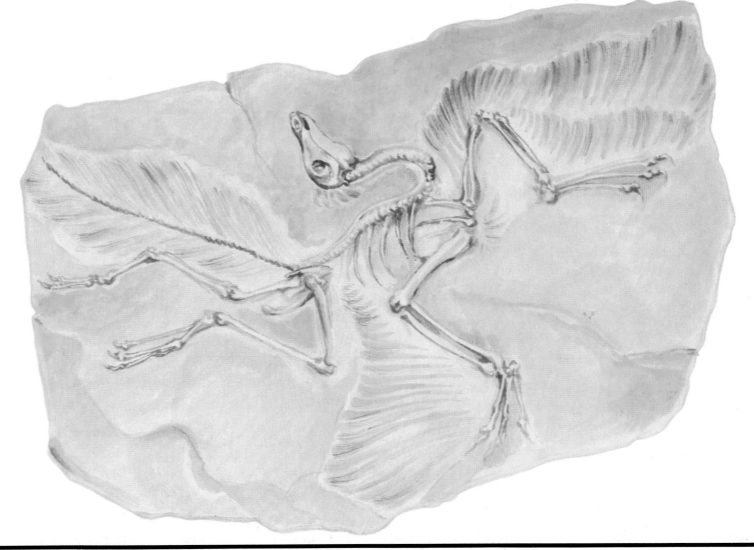

Sauropods

Were all the dinosaurs carnivores?

Sauropods (SORE-o-pods) were the gentle giants of the dinosaur world. Far from clumsy, Sauropods were built so that all of their parts moved together beautifully. With their tails held high and necks swaying back and forth through the trees, they seemed to glide through the forest. Because of their great size, a lot of people think that they were ferocious, but their spoon-shaped teeth tell a different story. Because they were short and dull, Sauropod teeth were good only for snipping the leaves off of trees. Besides, a Sauropod's small jaw could have done little harm to anything but a plant. They were herbivores (HERB-i-vors), which means they ate only green plants. Because green plants are stringy (like string beans) and hard to digest, Sauropods had specially large stomachs which made their bodies so huge. Compared to the rest of their bodies, Sauropods had little heads. Their breathing holes, or nostrils, were set high on their heads. This way they didn't have to stop eating to take a breath.

Brontosaurus

What can we find out from dinosaur footprints?

Six elephants put together would equal the size of one Brontosaurus (bron-to-SORE-us). Thick, straight legs full of muscles were needed to hold up all of those pounds. Each leg ended in five stubby toes buried in a round, padded foot.

The giant print made by one Brontosaurus foot would make a nice pool for a few babies to splash around in. From the designs made by the footprints, we can tell that Brontosaurus probably moved in groups or herds. Little footprints are surrounded by big footprints, telling us that the grownups protected the babies by making them stay within the herd.

Camarasaurus

Which Sauropod would be the easiest to tame?

If you could, by some magic, bring back one dinosaur to live in our world, Camarasaurus (ka-mar-a-SORE-us) would not be a bad choice. About half the size of Brontosaurus, she was gentle and easygoing.

She had no sharp teeth to tear apart her prey. The only things she ever attacked were plants—which she would swallow whole. Sometimes, she would eat a few big stones that would rub against each other in her stomach. The rubbing of the stones would help break up the unchewed plants just like your molars break up your food.

With Camarasaurus around, you wouldn't need a hedge clipper, but you would need a lot of hedges!

Brachiosaurus

Just how big did the dinosaurs get?

The biggest of the big, Brachiosaurus (brock-ee-o-SORE-us), was so large that if he didn't have such a great big neck and tail, he would have looked like a walking mountain. He probably weighed as much as eighty tons. That's as big as sixteen of the largest elephants you can find. With so many pounds to carry, it's no wonder that Brachiosaurus always stood on all four legs. He was just too heavy to lift his front legs up like his other Sauropod cousins. He needed a very strong heart in order to pump blood to his head and brain. It seems that he even had *two* brains: one in his head to help move his head and front legs and the other in his tail to help move his heavy rear end.

Diplodocus

Why did many of the dinosaurs have such long tails?

Diplodocus (di-PLOD-oke-us) was the longest of the Sauropods because of her whiplike tail. It would take only three of her to stretch all the way across a football field.

For Diplodocus, every day was a twenty-four-hour feast. Her long, graceful neck could drop way down to eat plants on the floor of the forest or she could weave in and out of the treetops like a giant hose. With such a long neck in front, she needed an equally long tail behind her to keep her body

balanced like a seesaw. We can tell that Sauropod tails were held high because there are no tailprints among the footprints. If an enemy came too close, she could scare him away with the great hooked claws on her front feet, or she could lash him to death with her powerful tail.

Did all the herbivores eat the same kinds of plants?

No. The right kind of menu for an Ornithopod (or-NITH-o-pod) would have lots of hard, thorny plants in it. If Ornithopods were around today, a cactus or two would probably make a nice snack. Just taking a bite out of one of these prickly plants would have been pretty hard to do if these Ornithopod dinosaurs didn't have specially hooked beaks to help them. All the teeth and muscles they had to help with so much chewing gave their cheeks a fat, puffed-up look like a chipmunk.

Camptosaurus

How big was Camptosaurus (camp-toe-SORE-us)?

Camptosaurus came in all different sizes. At his smallest, he was as big as an eight-year-old child. At his biggest, he would be able to look into your upstairs window. Like most Ornithopods, he usually walked on his hind legs, but his front legs were strong enough so he could drop down on all four feet. That way he could snap up all of those delicious, thorny tidbits on the forest floor.

Iguanodon

What do you do with a leftover bone?

When scientists first put Iguanodon's (ig-WAN-o-don) skeleton together, they didn't know what to do with the cone-shaped bone that they had left over. So they stuck it in the middle of the head like a rhinoceros. It wasn't until they found another skeleton of Iguanodon, this time all in one piece, that they found out that instead of having one bone too many, they actually had been missing a bone! Can you guess why? The answer is that Iguanodon was the proud owner of two built-in swords or cone-shaped bones which were stuck on the top of his thumbs. He probably used these weapons to poke out the eyes of his attackers.

Hadrosaurus

Can you imagine a dinosaur with a beak like a duck?

For years, scientists thought that because Hadrosaurus (Ha-dro-SORE-us) had a wide and flat beak like a duck's that he probably stayed in the water and ate the soft plants on the bottom of lakes.

That was before they found the Hadrosaurus mummy. Now, suppose an animal died and because of some special reasons like dry weather and protective layers of mud and sand, more than just a bony skeleton was left of her. Over the years, the animal's body would have turned to stone. That stone body is something like a mummy.

Inside the Hadrosaurus "mummy's" stomach were the kinds of plants that you would find on dry land. The legs were built for running, not swimming, and the feet had hooves, not webs.

Since ducks have no teeth, scientists were surprised to see that Hadrosaurus' jaws were lined with rows and rows of teeth—at least a thousand in all. When one tooth got worn down from eating too many hard plants, another one grew in its place.

Now, some scientists think that if you want to compare Hadrosaurus with an animal of today, an antelope would be a better choice.

Did you ever see a dinosaur wearing a hat? Standing next to his close relatives, the crested dinosaurs, Hadrosaurus must have looked pretty boring. They all had the same "duckbills" but the tops of their heads were something else again.

Parasaurolophus (par-a-sore-o-LO-fus) carried a hollow, curved tube that stretched past his head like a stiff ponytail.

Lambeosaurus (lam-bee-o-SORE-us) had a crest that looked like a tophat.

Parasaurolophus

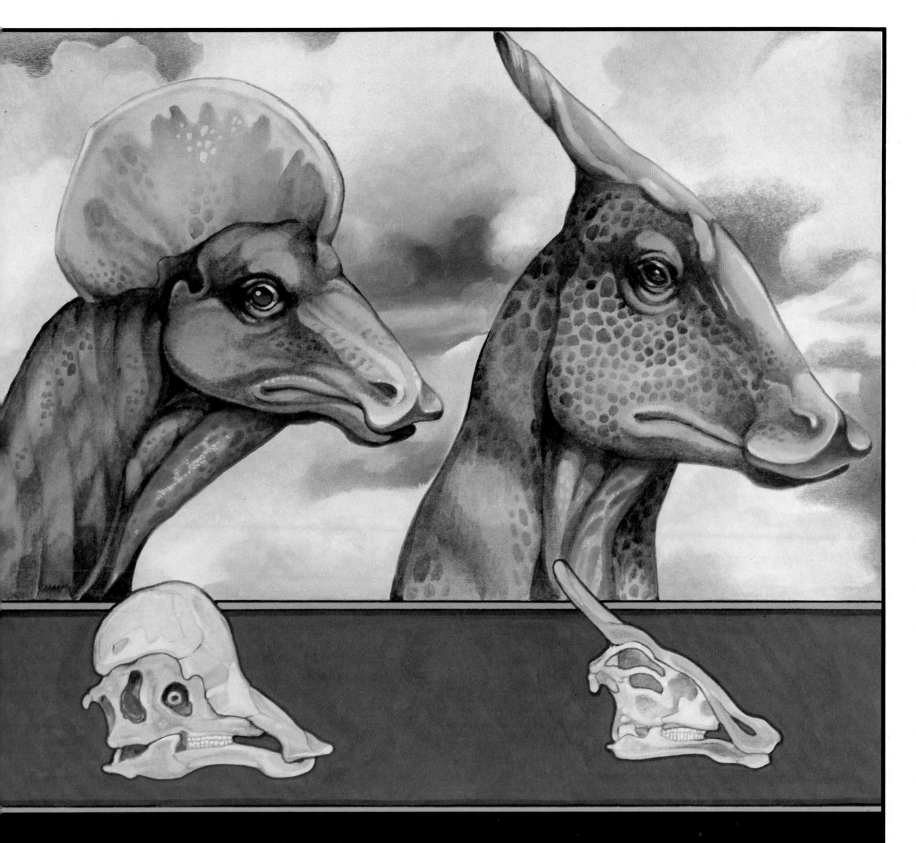

Corythosaurus' (ko-ree-o-SORE-us) crest looked like a helmet.

The crest worn by Saurolophus (sore-o-LO-fus) was twisted at the top like a pointed crown.

Some say that the crests were for breathing while the dinosaur hid or grazed underwater Others think they were just extra decorations. You must admit that the crested dinosaurs really looked special. Perhaps the crest was like a large nose that let the dinosaurs smell their prey from afar. Which idea do you think is best?

Corythosaurus

Saurolophus

Ceratopsian

What is a frill?

With their parrot beaks, thick-muscled necks, and horns growing out of their heads, Ceratopsians (ser-a-TOP-see-ans) would never have won any beauty contests. An eating contest would have been more appropriate. They had powerful jaws and grinding teeth that could mash up the toughest plants.

Your everyday Triceratops (tri-SER-uh-tops) was as long as two schoolbuses. Her head alone was the same length as the space between the floor and ceiling of your room. With a head that big, imagine what kind of neck she needed just to hold her head up! A normal neck just wouldn't do the trick. Something extra was needed. And that is where the frill came in (that long part of her head that looks like an upside-down saddle). It was chock-full of extra muscles and bones to help hold up that big head and move those enormous jaws. The three horns sticking out of her head right above her eyes were a good warning to her foe not to tangle with her.

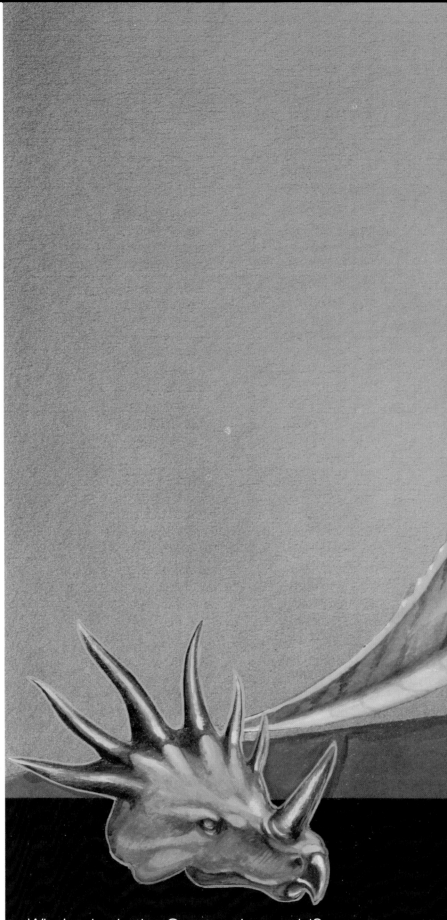

Who's who in the Ceratopsian world? Which dinosaur had the spiky frill?

Styracosaurus (sty-ra-co-SORE-us) had six long, sharp spikes decorating the edge of his frill.

Styracosaurus

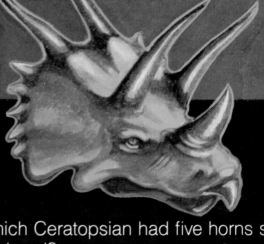

Which Ceratopsian had five horns sticking out of his head?

That's an easy one. Pentaceratops (penta-CER-a-tops), whose name means "five horns."

Which Ceratopsian had only one horn?

Monoclonius (mon-o-CLO-nee-us) had one horn on his nose like a rhinoceros.

Pentaceratops

Monoclonius

Protoceratops

Which Ceratopsian laid a nine-inch egg that looks like a giant jellybean?

None other than Protoceratops (pro-toe-SER-a-tops), one of the first Ceratopsians. Small for a Ceratopsian, a full-grown Protoceratops was only about as long as a small sports car.

Protoceratops laid the first dinosaur egg that was ever found. It was a nice-sized egg. She was probably satisfied with it. Can you believe that a lot of people were disappointed? They expected it to be at least as big as a football.

How did scientists know the egg belonged to Protoceratops?

Because the next egg they found had a little Protoceratops skeleton inside it. Right beside the egg was a newly hatched baby complete with frill! He was so small and helpless and had very tiny teeth. He must have needed a lot of care from his parents until he was old enough to be part of the herd.

Chasmosaurus

Which Ceratopsian had three horns and lots of holes in his frill?

Chasmosaurus (CHAS-muh-SAW-rus) had holes in his frill, but no one really knows why. He was the same size as a rhinoceros and could gallop as fast as a horse. Like many other animals, Ceratopsians would get into fights sometimes. Maybe when Ceratopsians fought each other their horns poked holes in each other's frills. Or maybe a solid frill was just too heavy for Chasmosaurus to carry around. A frill with holes would have been a lot lighter.

Stegosaurus

Why did the Stegosaurs (STEG-o-sores) have big, bony plates running down their backs? This is another question with many answers since scientists have many different ideas.

One idea is that Stegosaurs needed the plates for protection. Their weak teeth were of no help since they were made for chewing the soft, tender plants Stegosaurs liked best.

If a big carnivore tried to take a bite out of Stegosaur's back, those bony plates might just cause him to think twice about ruining his teeth.

Another idea is that the plates were only a decoration, and that the long spikes on the end of Stegosaur's tail would protect him from attack.

One new idea is that the plates on Stegosaur's back worked like a radiator in a car to help cool his body.

Can you think of any other ideas?

Kentrosaurus

Were Stegosaurus and Kentrosaurus as stupid as they looked?

For many years, scientists thought that dinosaurs were dumb and that the Stegosaurs, like Stegosaurus (steg-a-SORE-us) and Kentrosaurus (ken-tra-SORE-us), were the dumbest of them all. They figured that an animal with a little head and a tiny brain could not have been too smart.

Today, there are some scientists who think differently. They have given tests to crows, who have very small brains, and tests to dogs and cats, whose brains are much bigger. Guess who got the highest marks?

The crows, that's who. So maybe the size of your brain is not as important as what you do with it!

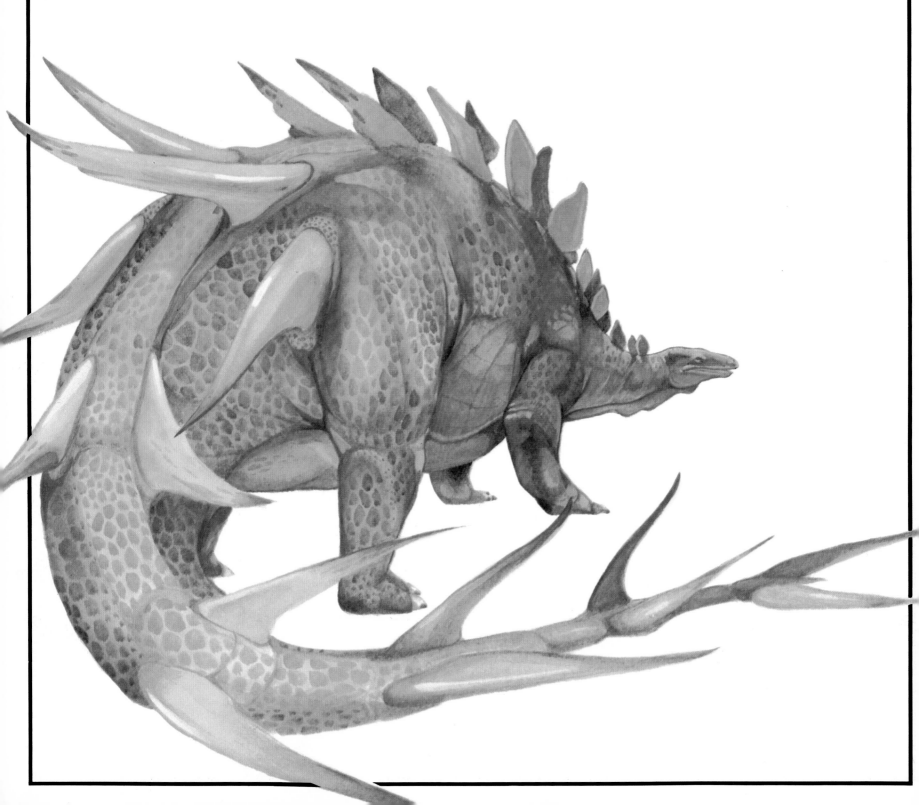

Ankylosaurus

Why was it hard for a big carnivore to get a taste of Ankylosaurus (an-kee-lo-SORE-us)?

Ankylosaurus had plates and spikes all over his chubby body. He weighed as much as an elephant, but was much shorter. He must have been a silly sight waddling along on his stubby legs.

About as tasty-looking as a porcupine, his bumpy body was ugly enough to turn off most carnivores. If one was particularly hungry, Ankylosaurus' tail made a pretty good club. Thick and powerful, it ended in a huge bone. As it swished back and forth, it could break some of the heaviest necks and legs in two. The best way to get a taste of Ankylosaurus meat was to flip him over on his back. His soft belly was just about the only place that had no armor to protect him.

When he was attacked, all he had to do was crouch down and tuck in his head, legs, tail, and hope for the best.

Allosaurus

Who were the bullies of the dinosaur world?

If an Allosaur (AL-lo-sore) dinosaur could read this book, his mouth would water. He would think it was a menu filled with all of his favorite treats. You see, he was put together to do three things best—to catch, kill, and eat other dinosaurs.

He had a mouth like a cave. His teeth were like icicles; but they worked like a saw to slice off huge pieces of meat and bone. His jaws had special bones that acted like hinges. They let him open up even wider to swallow enormous chunks of his latest catch.

What was Allosaurus' favorite meal?

One of the Allosaurs named Allosaurus loved Brontosaurus meat. Even though Brontosaurus was ten times his size, we know Allosaurus chased Brontosaurus because his three-toed footprints have been found inside the huge, bowl-shaped footprints of Brontosaurus. We know that Brontosaurus was caught because a Brontosaurus skeleton was discovered with teeth marks sunk into its backbone. Mixed in with these bones are the six-inch teeth of you know who.

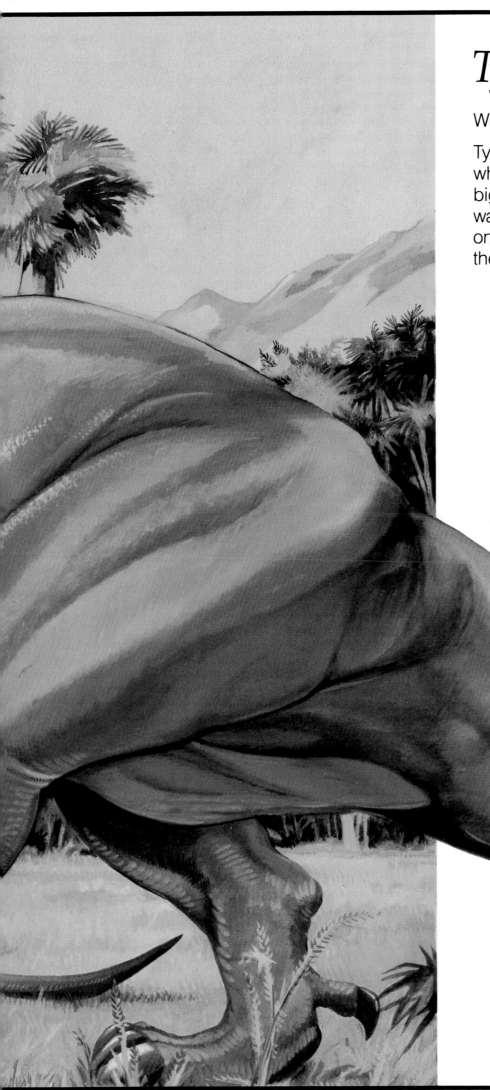

Tyrannosaurus Rex

What is the name of the biggest Allosaur?

Tyrannosaurus Rex (tie-ran-o-SORE-us Rex), which means "king of the tyrant lizards," was the biggest and most terrible killing-machine that ever walked the earth. He could swallow more meat in one mouthful than a human mother, father, and their child could eat in two months!

Deinonychus

Which Allosaur had the meanest temper?

Every part of Deinonychus' (dine-o-NYE-kus) body seemed to be put there for one reason—to make her an expert killer. Her strong hands had bendable wrists and thumbs to give her wonderful control over whatever she was holding in them. Each foot had a special super-sharp claw which could go in and out whenever Deinonychus needed to use it for stabbing. She had huge eyes which helped her to see very well and a large brain so that she could outsmart her prey.

She killed by holding an animal with her front claws while standing on one foot. Then, she kicked the animal to death with her other foot, using her special claw to tear it apart. Since she could control her long tail as well as a squirrel, she never lost her balance. She was only about as tall as a man, but some of the really big dinosaurs were afraid to go near her. Can you blame them?

What happened to the dinosaurs?

Dinosaurs lived on the earth longer than any other kind of animal. No other class of large animals, including human beings, even comes close. About 65,000,000 years ago, something must have happened to make the world a terrible place for dinosaurs.

The climate had been warm the way dinosaurs liked it. Then, a drastic change occurred. Many scientists think it became much colder so that the warm-blooded dinosaurs froze to death. Crocodiles and other small, cold-blooded creatures lived through the change by hibernating. Can you picture big, old Triceratops finding a cozy nest to curl up in until spring?

The latest idea is that a huge falling star crashed to the earth, making the world blazing hot like an oven. Smaller animals could perspire fast enough to cool their bodies. The dinosaurs could not do this, so they perished.

We have seen that dinosaurs were very good at making the changes needed to live well in their world. When the plants became tough, some dinosaurs grew bigger jaw muscles. When the plants grew tall, other dinosaurs grew very long necks.

The sudden change on earth was severe enough to wipe out these amazing animals that ruled the world for 140,000,000 years.

PENTACERATOPS

COELOPHYSIS

TYRANNOSAURUS REX

TRICERATOPS

CORYTHOSAURUS

ARCHAEOPTERYX

PARASAUROLOPHUS

ANKYLOSAURUS

COMPSOGNATHUS

ALLOSAURUS

DIPLODOCUS